Chapter 1

WITHDRAWN

"I wonder if Mom got peanut butter crackers," Emma Weber said as she, her brother Matthew, and her friend Katie Carew walked home after school on Wednesday afternoon.

"I love peanut butter crackers," Matthew said. "They would definitely make me feel better. Recess was bad today. I struck out in kickball."

Katie understood. Striking out in kickball was a big deal when you were in first grade.

"Peanut butter makes all your troubles disappear," she told him.

Suddenly, the kids heard some loud yelling from Emma W.'s backyard.

"*Let's get rough! Let's get mean! Let's roll over the other team!*"

"That's Lacey and her friend Rachel," Emma W. explained. "They're practicing for a cheerleading competition."

"They're *always* practicing," Matthew said. "And they practice really loud."

"You're so lucky to have a sister who is a high school cheerleader," Katie told Emma W.

"Yes," Emma W. agreed. "And Lacey is really good at it. It's just that . . ."

"Lacey never *stops* cheering," Matthew said, finishing his sister's sentence.

As the kids headed into the Webers' backyard, Lacey and her friend started a new cheer.

"*You might be good at baseball or running 'round a track. But when it comes to basketball, you'd better jump back!*" the girls shouted. Then they leaped up in the air with their arms and legs spread apart. "Go Cherrydale!"

"Wow!" Katie exclaimed. "That was awesome."

Lacey shook her head. "No, it wasn't," she said. "We didn't land at the same time, and Rachel's right leg was crooked."

"It was not," Rachel told Lacey. "It was a perfect X jump." Rachel looked over at Emma W., Katie, and Matthew. "Wasn't it?"

Katie had no idea what an X jump was. So she just said, "I thought it looked good."

"Here it comes," Matthew said quietly.

"*Good* isn't good enough," Lacey said angrily. "This cheer has to be absolutely perfect. We're going to be in a statewide competition. We can't win if we're just *good*."

Oops. Katie frowned. Maybe *good* was the wrong word to use.

"I meant exciting," Katie said. But Rachel and Lacey weren't listening to Katie anymore.

"Let's do it again," Lacey told Rachel. She pulled her red and white pom-poms to her chest.

As Lacey and Rachel started the cheer again, Katie followed Emma W. and her little brother into the house.

"I am so sick of hearing cheers," Matthew groaned as he threw his backpack onto the kitchen counter.

Katie understood. A few months ago, her mom had started taking tap-dancing classes, and she went nuts practicing.

"I wish Lacey would stop cheering forever!" Matthew exclaimed.

Uh-oh. Matthew had just made a wish. That was *sooo* not good. Wishes could be trouble. No one knew that better than Katie.

Chapter 2

It had all started back in third grade on one really, *really* rotten day. First, Katie had missed the football and lost the game for her team. Then she'd fallen in the mud and ruined her favorite pair of jeans. And then, just when she thought things couldn't get any worse, she'd let out a burp in front of the whole class. And not just any burp. A *huge* burp. *A real record breaker.*

That night, Katie had wished she could be anyone but herself. There must have been a shooting star flying overhead when Katie made her wish, because the next day the magic wind came. The magic wind was a wild, powerful tornado that blew just around Katie. It was so strong that it could blow her right out of her own body and into someone else's.

The first time the magic wind came it turned her into Speedy, the class hamster. Katie had spent the whole morning stuck in a cage. She was really glad the magic wind returned to switch her back into her own body before her friends realized it was Katie on that hamster wheel, wearing nothing but hamster fur!

The magic wind came back again and again after that. It turned Katie into lots of people and animals. And every time Katie switcherooed, she really made a mess of things.

Like the time the magic wind switcherooed Katie into a hairdresser named Sparkle. Katie didn't know the first thing about cutting hair, so just turning into a hairdresser would have been bad enough. What made it worse was that Katie's best friend, Suzanne Lock, was the person getting her hair cut. Boy, did Katie make a mess out of Suzanne's head!

Sometimes Katie's switcheroos could be pretty gross. Once she turned into a reindeer with big, hairy lips. Another time she became her class snake, Slinky, just as he was shedding his skin.

The magic wind was the reason Katie didn't make wishes anymore. She knew what kinds of weird things could happen if they came true.

But Matthew didn't know that. And Katie wasn't going to tell him. He wouldn't believe her, anyway. So instead, Katie just said, "You don't really wish that, Matthew."

"Katie's right," Emma W. added. "Cheerleading makes Lacey happy. We want her to be happy."

"I guess," Matthew agreed. "But why can't she be quieter while she's being happy?"

Emma W. laughed. "Hey, let's see if Mom got peanut butter crackers," she said.

"Mom!" Matthew called out. "Do we have any crackers?"

Mrs. Weber came running out from the laundry room. "Matthew, you know not to yell when the twins are taking a nap," she scolded.

"Sorry," Matthew apologized. "I'm very hungry."

"School can do that to you," Mrs. Weber said with a smile. "Hi, Katie," she added. "I didn't even hear you kids come in."

"You can't hear anything with Lacey cheering so loudly," Matthew complained.

Mrs. Weber laughed and handed out peanut butter crackers to each of the kids.

Just then, Katie heard some loud crying coming from upstairs.

Emma W. frowned. "I guess Tyler and Timmy are done with their naps."

Mrs. Weber sighed. "I'd better go change them."

"Wah! Wah!" the twins cried.

"I'm coming, boys," Mrs. Weber shouted.

"D-D-D-Defense, take that ball away!" Lacey and Rachel cheered from the backyard.

Wow. It sure was noisy at Emma W.'s house. It was never like this at Katie's house. Katie didn't have brothers or sisters. It was just her, her parents, and her dog, Pepper. It was usually pretty quiet at the Carews' house, and most of the time that was nice. In fact, it was pretty great being Katie Carew—when the magic wind let her stay that way.

Chapter 3

"Everybody on your feet! Cherrydale High can't be beat. Dribble it. Pass it. We scored a basket! Go Cherrydale High!"

Katie leaped up into the air and bent her right knee, sort of like the jump Rachel had done the day before. Emma W. spun around and shook her hands in the air, pretending she was waving pom-poms.

"You guys are so cool," Miriam Chan said.

A bunch of girls were in the school yard, watching Katie and Emma W. before school began.

"Good jump, Katie Kazoo," Mandy Banks

said, using the way-cool nickname Katie's friend George had given her back in third grade.

Katie nodded. "It's hard doing that."

Zoe Canter jumped up in the air and gave it a try. *Oomph.* Instead of landing on her feet, she landed on her rear end. "I see what you mean."

"You almost had it," Emma W. assured Zoe.

Just then, Suzanne walked over to where the girls were all standing.

"I'm so glad everyone is here," Suzanne said. "Look! I have a new leopard-print backpack." She turned around so everyone could see it.

But the girls were all too busy talking about cheerleading to care about Suzanne's backpack.

"You remember that funny basketball cheer?" Katie asked.

"Oh yeah," Emma W. said. *"Salt makes you thirsty and pepper makes you sneeze . . ."*

"When it comes to shooting baskets, we drive you to your knees," Katie said, finishing the cheer.

"What's so funny about that?" Suzanne said. "I think it's dumb. What do salt and pepper have to do with basketball, anyway?"

"It's just a rhyme," Katie told her. "And it's got a good beat."

"Since when are you and Emma W. cheerleaders?" Suzanne said.

"We're not," Katie said.

"My sister is," Emma W. explained. She leaped up and did a split in midair. Her back leg was bent but her front leg was straight.

"That's called a herkie," Emma W. said.

"It looked kind of *jerky* to me," Suzanne said. "Now, my backpack, that's *really* something to cheer about."

"Sure. Whatever," Mandy said.

"Do they ever do flips or cartwheels in their cheers?" Becky asked Emma W.

"I think so," Emma W. said. "They're working on new routines because there's a big statewide competition coming up."

"Teach us a cheer," Zoe said.

"The defense cheer is pretty easy," Emma W. told the girls. "It's mostly clapping and stamping your feet."

All the girls lined up behind Emma W. Well, almost all the girls. Suzanne never lined up *behind* anyone. She liked to be in front.

"D-D-D-Defense! D-D-D-Defense!" Emma W. and Katie shouted out.

"D-D-D-Defense!" the other girls cheered back.

Suzanne stomped off angrily toward the school building.

Uh-oh. Katie knew for sure that Suzanne would find *some way* to make sure everyone was paying attention to her again.

And that meant a good D-D-D-Defense was exactly what Katie was going to need.

Chapter 4

"*Can't wait for the bell to ring. Makes my hips start to swing. School rules! Yay school!*"

Katie walked into the school yard the next day just in time to see Suzanne leading a cheer. Behind her were Becky, Miriam, and Zoe. They were wearing white shirts with the number *4* and the letter *B* in red felt pinned to the front. They each held a pair of white, plastic pom-poms.

"We're the 4B pom-pom squad," Suzanne informed Katie. "I'm the captain."

"Cool," Katie said. "Can I join?"

Suzanne rolled her eyes. "You obviously didn't hear me, Katie. I said we're the 4*B* pom-pom squad. You're in 4*A*."

Katie looked at Suzanne. It was clear that Suzanne was still really mad at Katie for taking all the attention away from her backpack yesterday. Katie didn't understand why Suzanne always made such a big deal out of little things.

"Suzanne, sometimes you can be such a baby," she said.

"Can a baby do this?" Suzanne jumped up and bent her back leg, just the way Katie had done yesterday. Only, instead of landing on her feet, she tripped over her shoelace and slammed into a tree. "Ouch," Suzanne groaned.

"Are you okay?" Katie asked.

"Of course," Suzanne said. "I *meant* to do that."

Somehow Katie doubted that. But Suzanne wasn't as hurt as Katie was. Starting a pom-pom squad that Katie couldn't be on was so mean. And Suzanne had definitely meant to do *that*.

★ ★ ★

"Get that Jell-O, grab some meat! 4B's eaters are hard to beat!"

Katie heard Suzanne and the rest of the 4B pom-pom squad cheering as soon as she walked into the cafeteria. They were cheering while the 4B boys piled food onto their trays.

"A cheer for lunch?" Emma W. asked Katie.

"*Take a milk or maybe juice! When it comes to lunch, 4B can't lose.*" Suzanne waved her pom-poms in the air as she cheered wildly.

"Why is she doing this?" Emma W. asked.

"Why does Suzanne do *anything*?" Mandy asked.

"I don't know," Katie admitted. "But I can't wait until she stops."

All day, no matter where Katie went, the 4B pom-pom squad was cheering about something.

On her way to the bathroom, Katie heard a cheer coming from the 4B classroom:

"Manny, Manny, he's our man. If he can't divide, no one can!"

And then, when 4A played 4B in volleyball, the girls in 4B kept shouting:

"Bump it. Set it. Spike it! That's the way we like it! Go class 4B!"

Some of the 4B pom-pom girls even cheered during band practice.

"Jeremy's got the beat, gonna bring us to our feet," Becky shouted. *"Other instruments are just plain dumb. Come on, Jeremy, bang that drum!"*

Kevin Camilleri laughed. "Yeah, Jeremy," he said in a high, girly voice. "Bang that drum." He batted his eyelashes up and down.

"Kevin, cut it out," Jeremy said.

Katie felt bad for Jeremy. Everyone knew Becky had a huge crush on him.

Katie was really glad when Mr. Starkey said, "Becky, no instrument in a band is dumb. They're all equally important."

"Well, some are more equal than others," Becky said.

"That doesn't even make sense," Kevin told Becky. "*Equal* means all the same."

"Exactly," Mr. Starkey said. "And as far as I'm concerned, every musician in this band is a star. So let's make some music!"

Katie was very happy to pick up her clarinet and start playing the opening to the band's new song, "Doo Wah Diddy Diddy." The music would definitely drown out any cheering.

At least for now.

* * *

"Hurry up, Katie," Jeremy urged as Katie left school at the end of the day. "I don't want Suzanne and the rest of the pom-pom squad to follow me home."

"Suzanne's making you nuts, too?" Katie asked as she and Jeremy turned the corner and headed down the block.

"It's awful," Jeremy said. "They were actually cheering for Sam McDonough when he went into the bathroom."

Katie made a face. She didn't even want to think about what *that* one sounded like.

"Doesn't Suzanne ever cheer for any of the

girls?" Katie asked Jeremy.

He shook his head. "She can't," he said.

"Why not?" Katie asked him.

"Because all of the girls in our class are on the 4B pom-pom squad," Jeremy explained. "That just leaves us guys to cheer for."

Unfortunately, Katie sort of felt like all the problems in class 4B were her fault. After all, she was the one who had been cheering in the school yard yesterday. But Katie and Emma W. had just been having fun. They weren't trying to drive people crazy or anything.

Driving people crazy was more of a Suzanne thing. And she did it better than anyone.

Chapter 5

The next day at school was no better. As class 4A walked down the hall to the library, class 4B was heading toward the art room. Suzanne started to wave her pom-poms the minute she spotted Katie and Emma W.

"Grab that brush. Add some paint. If it's not 4B art, then art it ain't!" the 4B pom-pom squad cheered.

"*Ain't* isn't even a word," Mandy said.

"Exactly," Kadeem Carter agreed. "*Ain't* ain't a word 'cause *ain't* ain't in the dictionary!"

Katie giggled. Kadeem could be pretty funny sometimes.

Luckily, Ms. Sweet, class 4B's teacher, knew how to stop the cheering. "Girls," she scolded. "That's not how we behave in school."

"Sorry," Miriam, Becky, Zoe, and Jessica Haynes all said at once.

But Suzanne started to cheer all over again. *"Sorry, sorry is what I am! No one is sorrier than Suzanne."*

Kevin groaned. "She's sorry, all right. A sorry excuse for a cheerleader!"

Katie hated when her friends said mean things about one another. But Suzanne was taking this whole cheerleading thing way too far.

"Hey, Katie, do you want to come over after school today?" Emma W. asked as the girls walked into the library.

Katie didn't know what to say. She really didn't want to spend another afternoon listening to Lacey and Rachel practicing cheers. "Do you want to come to my house instead?" Katie suggested.

Emma W. shook her head. "I can't," she

said. "My mom needs someone to keep an eye on Matthew while she's taking care of the twins. And since Lacey has an after-school cheerleading practice, that someone is me."

Katie smiled. Lacey wasn't going to be home.

"Sure, I'll come over," Katie said. "I'll call my mom later from the school office."

Things were nice and quiet at Emma W.'s house that afternoon. Mrs. Weber was in the living room playing blocks with Timmy and Tyler. Katie and Emma W. were in the backyard finger-painting with Matthew. It was a warm, spring day, so it was nice to be outside.

"Wow, Matthew," Katie said. "I like the purple dog you painted."

"That's an elephant," Matthew told her. "I just didn't add the trunk yet."

"Oh," Katie said. "Sorry. Now I can see. It's definitely an elephant."

Katie dipped her fingers in the brown paint and started to paint a picture of Pepper. She started with his big, brown eyes, and then worked her way back to his stubby, little tail.

Finger painting wasn't the kind of thing she would usually do with a friend because it was a first-grade thing, not a fourth-grade thing. But since Matthew was in first grade, Katie and Emma W. had an excuse. And if someone said it was babyish—someone like *Suzanne*, for instance—the girls could just say that they were finger-painting to make Matthew happy.

"Would you pass the yellow?" Emma W. asked Katie.

Katie looked over at her friend's paper. "Nice rainbow," she said as she passed the yellow.

"Thanks," Emma W. said. "I'm so glad Mr. G. gave us that little trick to remember what order the colors go in."

Katie knew exactly what trick Emma W. was talking about. They'd learned it on the day they were studying light. Mr. G. had come to school dressed in a rainbow shirt, with a rainbow-colored wig on his head. He had told everyone his name was Roy G. Biv.

Except Roy G. Biv wasn't a real person. Roy G. Biv was the way Mr. G. wanted them to remember the colors in the rainbow: red, orange, yellow, green, blue, indigo, violet.

"Mr. G. is a very cool teacher," Katie said.

"The coolest," Emma W. agreed, smushing some yellow paint around on her paper.

Katie reached for the red paint so she could start making Pepper's collar. But before she could dip her hand into the dish, Lacey and Rachel came racing into the backyard.

"You guys have to leave," Lacey told them.

"Why?" Emma W. asked her sister.

"Because our squad learned a new cheer today and we have to practice so that we can do it perfectly at the game on Saturday," Lacey told her.

"We were here first," Matthew said.

"Well now you're leaving first," Lacey said. "Mom said we have to practice out here. The ceilings are too low for us to do our jumps in the house."

"But mom said she didn't want us painting inside," Emma W. explained. "It makes too much of a mess."

"Then do something else," Lacey told her.

"Can't we share the yard?" Katie asked.

Lacey shook her head. "No way. We need a lot of room."

Katie couldn't believe what she was hearing. Lacey was acting like she owned the backyard. And that wasn't true.

But Emma W. was already packing up the paints and paper. She obviously didn't feel like arguing with her sister.

"It's getting a little chilly, anyway," Emma W. told Katie and Matthew.

Katie had been happy to be finger-painting. And she'd been happy not having to hear cheers for a while. "I don't know why you guys have to practice so much," Katie told Lacey and Rachel. "Cheerleading isn't *that* hard."

"Are you kidding?" Rachel demanded.

"Cheerleaders are athletes!" Lacey said. "We have to practice, just like in any sport."

"There's no cheerleading in the Olympics," Katie told her.

Lacey and Rachel just stared at Katie. They couldn't believe what she had just said.

"You don't know anything," Lacey told Katie.

But Katie *did* know something. She knew she hated cheerleading. Cheerleading had ruined her day in school, and now it was ruining her playdate after school.

Cheerleading was definitely *not* something to cheer about. No way!

Chapter 6

"But, Katie, you just *have* to come with me," Emma W. pleaded that night on the phone. "I don't want to sit at that basketball game without a friend to talk to."

Katie sighed. She really liked Emma W. A lot. But she really didn't want to go to the high school basketball game tomorrow.

"My mom has to take Matthew and the twins for their doctor's appointments," Emma W. explained. "She said I could go to the game if a friend sits in the bleachers with me. Otherwise I have to go with her. And I hate going to the doctor's. Even if it's not for me."

Katie didn't blame Emma W. Going to the

doctor's was no fun. There was always a little kid crying after getting a shot or someone sneezing and coughing all over the place.

"Okay," Katie said finally. "I'll go with you."

"Katie, you're the best!" Emma W. said.

"I've never actually been to a high school basketball game," Katie admitted.

"The Cherrydale High team is good," Emma W. said. "They haven't lost a game all season."

As Katie hung up the phone, she smiled. It was very grown-up to go to a high school basketball game.

Katie wasn't even going to look at mean old Lacey Weber and the other cheerleaders. She was going to watch the basketball players. They were the *real* athletes, after all!

⭐ ⭐ ⭐

"Let's go Squids! Let's GO!" The crowd in the Cherrydale High School gym cheered as the basketball players raced across the court at the start of the game.

"Who named our team the *Squids*?" Katie

asked Emma W. They were staring at somebody who was dressed up in a red and white squid costume. It was pretty funny-looking, with bulging red eyes, a white belly, and eight red arms.

"How does he see in there?" Katie wondered.

"I think there are holes underneath that thing that looks like a snout," Emma W. said.

The mascot was twirling around and shaking his huge tentacles all over the place.

Then two players stood facing each other at the center of the court. The ref blew the whistle, tossed up the basketball, and the game began. It was exciting to watch. The Squids scored first, and then almost right away the same player threw the ball from miles away. *Swish!* In the hoop it went.

Katie pretty much avoided Lacey and the other cheerleaders each time the Squids scored another basket.

Soon the score was 22–19. The Cherrydale High School Squids were ahead. But that could change any minute.

BUZZZ! Before anyone else could score a basket, the buzzer rang. The players all raced off the court.

"Where are they going?" Katie asked.

"It's halftime," Emma W. explained. "The players go into the locker rooms for a rest."

"What do we do while they're resting?" Katie asked her.

"We watch the halftime show," Emma W. said. "The cheerleaders from both schools do some of their best cheers. They try to keep the crowd really excited."

"Um, Emma W.," Katie asked. "Do you mind if I go get some candy in the lobby?"

"No," Emma W. replied. "I'll wait here so no one takes our seats."

"Cool," Katie said. "I'll be right back."

And with that, Katie climbed down the bleachers and headed out a nearby door. She found herself in a hallway outside the gym. Katie turned a corner, looking for the candy machines. What she found instead were a bunch of classrooms facing a wall of lockers. Katie was a little nervous. The high school was big— much bigger than the elementary school. It would be easy for a fourth-grader to get lost.

Just then, Katie felt a breeze blowing on the back of her neck. That was weird. There were no windows in this hallway and all the doors to the classrooms were closed. So where was that breeze coming from?

A moment later, the wind started blowing harder and harder—just around Katie. That could only mean one thing: This was no ordinary wind. This was the *magic* wind! *Oh no!*

The magic wind began to blow more and more wildly until it was circling Katie like a fierce tornado. The wind was so powerful, Katie thought she might be blown away! She shut her eyes tight and tried really hard not to cry.

And then it stopped. Just like that. The magic wind was gone.

And so was Katie Carew. She'd been turned into someone else. One . . . two . . . switcheroo!

But who?

Chapter 7

All around Katie, people were shouting and cheering. The air smelled of sweaty sneakers and floor wax. Slowly, she opened her eyes. She could see people sitting in the bleachers on either side of her. Up on the wall there was a sign. It said SQUIDS 22, VISITORS 19.

Okay, so the magic wind had blown Katie back into the Cherrydale High School gym. Now Katie knew *where* she was. But she still didn't know *who* she was.

Slowly she looked down. Her red, high-top sneakers were gone. Instead, Katie was wearing a pair of plain white sneakers with red laces and red socks.

And she wasn't wearing her cool new jeans with the flowers embroidered on the pockets anymore. Katie was wearing a little red and white skirt. A *cheerleading* skirt!

Uh-oh! That could only mean one thing. The magic wind had switcherooed Katie into one of the Cherrydale High cheerleaders, right in the middle of the halftime show!

"Come on, Lacey," Katie heard one of the cheerleaders say. "Grab your pom-poms."

Katie looked around for Lacey.

"Lacey, quit looking around. Grab your pom-poms and get into formation for the salt-and-pepper cheer," Rachel said.

Suddenly Katie realized that the cheerleaders were staring right at her. They were all holding red and white pom-poms. But Katie wasn't. *Uh-oh*. Katie knew what that had to mean.

The magic wind had switcherooed Katie into Lacey Weber!

It seemed like everyone in the gym was waiting for her to line up.

But Katie couldn't move. Her feet were glued to the floor.

"Lacey," Rachel whispered. "What's wrong?"

What was wrong was that Lacey was really Katie. But of course Katie couldn't tell Rachel that. She couldn't tell *anybody* that.

Katie bent down and grabbed her pom-poms. Then she took a deep breath and took her place behind Rachel in the formation.

Maybe this would turn out okay. After all, she knew all of the steps to the salt-and-pepper cheer. Well, *pretty much* all of the steps, anyway.

"Salt and pepper," the cheerleading captain shouted. "Ready? And . . ."

"Salt makes you thirsty and pepper makes you sneeze. When it comes to shooting baskets, we drive you to your knees!" Katie shouted out along with everybody else. She tried to do the same moves as the other cheerleaders. She shook her pom-poms to the right. Then she shook them to the left. Unfortunately, the other cheerleaders were shaking their pom-poms to the *left* and then to the *right*.

Katie twirled around and shook her pom-poms in the air.

The other cheerleaders twirled around and shook their pom-poms down low.

Katie leaped up in the air and did an X jump.

The other cheerleaders dropped to their knees and waved their pom-poms all around.

"What was that all about?" Rachel hissed in Katie's ear as the cheer ended.

"Quit trying to change the routine," Tess, the squad captain, whispered in Katie's ear.

"I wasn't . . . ," Katie began. But Tess didn't hear her. She'd already walked away and started the next cheer.

"Okay, pyramid formation!" Tess called out to the other cheerleaders. "Ready? Begin!"

Almost instantly, the cheerleaders began to form their pyramid. Four girls got on their hands and knees. They were the bottom row. Three more girls began climbing onto their backs. Katie hurried over, and started to climb on, too.

"What are you doing, Lacey?" Rachel asked. "You're the one on top, remember?"

Katie gulped. The top? Already, two girls were climbing onto the backs of the three girls on the second level of the pyramid. That meant Katie was going to have to climb over those girls and stand all the way at the top of the pyramid. And that was really, really high up.

This was *soooo* not good!

Chapter 8

"Lacey, what are you waiting for?" Tess said. She sounded annoyed. "Come on."

A cheerleader in the bottom row said, "Hurry up. My back is killing me."

But the pyramid was too high and scary to climb up. There was only so much a fourth-grade girl could do—even if that fourth-grade girl was stuck inside a high school cheerleader's body.

Now there was laughing coming from the other side of the gym floor. The Stallions' cheerleaders were pointing at her.

"That squad is the worst," one of them said, loud enough for Katie to hear. "We'll definitely beat those losers at the state competition."

Now Katie felt really bad. The Cherrydale High cheerleaders were not losers. They were really good—at least they were when Katie wasn't on their squad.

"I'll show them!" Katie cheered quietly to herself. She put her foot on the back of one of the cheerleaders on the bottom row and began to climb up the pyramid.

Slowly, Katie managed to climb over the first girl, then hoist herself over to the next row. So far so good. Katie took a deep breath and told herself not to look down. Grabbing on to Rachel's shoulders,

Katie somehow scrambled her way to the top and, trying not to wobble, Katie stood up as tall as she could. Then she spread her arms up in a *V* for victory.

"I did it!" Katie shouted. "I did . . . WHOA!"

Katie went flying backward off the pyramid, waving her arms wildly up and down as she fell. *Oof!* A moment later Katie landed right on her rear end. *Ouch!*

Crash! Katie wasn't the only one falling. The girls in the pyramid were knocked to either side as Katie fell. They all hit the ground.

Everyone in the gym started laughing— including the Cherrydale High fans.

"Lacey! What is the matter with you?" Tess, the team captain, hissed.

Suddenly tears started falling from Katie's eyes. She just couldn't stay in the gym another minute. And so she did a very fourth-grade girl kind of thing.

She took off and ran. She ran past the squid who was laughing so hard, he was rolling

around on the
floor. She didn't
stop running
until she
couldn't hear
any laughter.
By then, she
was completely lost
somewhere in the huge high school.

Suddenly, Katie felt a cool breeze blowing on
the back of her neck. She looked around for an
open window. But there weren't any.

That could only mean one thing. This was no
ordinary wind. This was the magic wind. It was
back!

The magic wind got stronger and stronger
after that. It began whipping around wildly, like
a powerful tornado. A tornado that was only
spinning around Katie. It was blowing so hard,
Katie was afraid it might blow her all the way to
the real pyramids—in Egypt!

And then it stopped. Just like that. The magic

wind was gone. Katie Kazoo was back!

So was Lacey. And, boy, did she look confused!

"What am I doing here?" she asked Katie.

That was a hard question to answer. "Everyone was laughing, so I had to . . . I mean *you* had to . . ."

Lacey got a funny look on her face. "I ran out of the gym," she said slowly. "Because everyone was laughing at me. I sort of remember. It's all kind of fuzzy."

Katie frowned. She felt terrible about what had just happened in the gym. "Well, they weren't just laughing at you," she told Lacey. "The whole pyramid fell."

"Because of me," Lacey said. She shook her head. "I don't know what happened. One minute I was up there, and the n—"

"You were down on the floor," Katie said, finishing her sentence.

"Yeah," Lacey said. She rubbed her rear end. "I don't know how I lost my balance."

"It's not your fault," Katie told her. "You were up really high. It's a very difficult trick."

Lacey shook her head. "Katie, how would you know?" she said.

"I know. Believe me," Katie said. "I'm sorry for what I said the other day. Being a cheerleader takes a lot of skill."

"That's okay." Then Lacey gave Katie a funny look. "What are you doing out here, anyway?"

Oh man. How could Katie explain that?

"I . . . um . . . well . . . I was looking for the candy machines and I made a wrong turn," she said.

"A majorly wrong turn," Lacey said. She stood up. "Come on. We'll go get Emma and walk back to our house."

"But you can't leave," Katie told her. "The game's only half over. You still have cheers to do."

"I'm not going back," Lacey said. "I don't want to be laughed at again."

"But you can't quit," Katie said. "Your team needs you."

"It's called a squad," Lacey corrected her.

"Same thing," Katie said. "You're the one who told me that cheerleaders were athletes, remember?"

Lacey shrugged. "I guess. But what does that have to do with anything?"

"Well, real athletes don't quit," Katie told her. "They keep playing until the game is over. So if you're a real athlete . . ."

"I'll go back in there and keep cheering," Lacey said, standing up and finishing the sentence. "You know, you're pretty smart for a fourth-grader."

Katie smiled. That was a big compliment— especially from a high school teenager. Lacey was actually a nice person. At least she was when she didn't have pom-poms in her hands.

Chapter 9

When Lacey returned to the gym, all the other cheerleaders refused to talk to her. They kept shooting her dirty looks behind her back.

Katie couldn't believe it. "Those girls are being really mean to your sister," Katie said once she returned to her seat in the bleachers with the candy she bought in the lobby. She handed Emma W. one of the two packages of red licorice she had. "It's not fair."

"I know," Emma W. said. "Anyone can make a mistake."

"Exactly," Katie said.

"The thing is," Emma W. continued, "Lacey's been on top of the pyramid a whole bunch of

times, and she's never fallen. So why today?"

Katie frowned. She knew why. But of course she could never explain it to Emma W.

"The other cheerleaders will get over it," Katie said hopefully. "By the end of the game they'll probably forget all about what happened."

★ ★ ★

But that wasn't what happened. In fact, right after the game, the cheerleading coach asked the girls to stay for a squad meeting. Katie and Emma W. could hear everything she was saying from where they were sitting on the bleachers. They were waiting for Lacey to walk home. But that was going to have to wait.

"I videotaped your whole performance," she told the squad. "Watching the tape will help us figure out what went wrong so we can fix it before the big competition next week."

Katie glanced over at Lacey. She looked a little sick to her stomach. It was obvious she didn't want to watch what had happened during the halftime show.

Neither did Katie.

"Hey, Emma W., do you want to go to my house for a while?" Katie asked her friend. "I can call my dad. Maybe he'll pick us up now."

Emma W. shook her head. "I promised my mom I would stay with Lacey," she explained. "But you can go home if you want to."

"No, it's okay," Katie said. "I'll stay here with you."

Katie and Emma W. followed the older girls into their locker room. They sat in the back of the room and waited for the coach to set up the video.

"Okay, now see how wonderfully you guys were doing the defense cheer in the first quarter?" the coach asked the girls. "Your rhythm is perfect. And every single herkie is championship quality."

Katie felt herself relax a little. Maybe this wouldn't be so bad after all.

"But things definitely went downhill during the halftime performance," the coach continued.

"Downhill is one word for it," Tess said. "Down *pyramid* is another."

Lacey turned beet red.

Katie couldn't believe it. "That girl is acting like she's never made any mistakes," she whispered to Emma W.

"Come on now, Tess," the coach said. "Anyone can have an off day. Let's watch the video and learn from our mistakes."

"They weren't *our* mistakes," another cheerleader said. "They were *Lacey's*."

Okay, now Katie was really mad. That was meaner than mean!

Katie stared at the video of the girls beginning their pyramid formation.

"Your timing was off, Lacey," the coach said. "The pyramid needs to be built really quickly."

"I know," Lacey said. "I don't understand why I was just standing there."

On the TV screen, Katie watched herself spread out her arms and shout, "I did it! I did . . ."

And then . . . WHOA!

The cheerleaders all started laughing. All except Lacey. She looked like she wanted to cry.

"No! Wait! That could be a great move," Katie shouted out.

"Oh, Katie, not now . . . ," Lacey began.

"No, seriously," Katie said, turning to face the squad. "Didn't you guys see how I . . . I mean how *Lacey* went backward in the air? And then when everyone fell out of the pyramid, they sort of made a V shape. You know, like *V* for victory?"

Katie stopped and took a deep breath. She waited for someone to say something.

"With a little more practice, that could be an amazing trick," Katie said. "At least, that's how it looks to me."

At first, no one spoke. And then Rachel said, "The kid's right. We did kind of make a *V*."

"Jumping off backward *is* kind of cool," Tess told Lacey. "Well, except for all the arm flapping you were doing. Were you trying to fly or something?"

Lacey laughed in spite of herself. "I have no idea what I was doing."

"If you girls can clean this routine up, we might have a championship-winning pyramid," the coach told them. "But it would take a lot of work—especially on your part, Lacey."

"I'll do whatever it takes," Lacey said.

"The state competition is only a week away," the coach reminded everyone.

"Then we should start practicing now," Lacey said, grabbing her pom-poms.

As Lacey and the other cheerleaders raced back into the gym to begin practicing, Emma

W. turned to Katie. "You really saved the day for my sister," she said. "Thanks."

Katie smiled. "It wasn't a big deal."

Emma W. said, "You have no idea what Lacey can be like when she's upset. It was a *huge* deal." To prove it, Emma W. raised her arms high in the air. *"K-A-T-I-E! Katie is the friend for me!"*

Chapter 10

"Hey, do you guys want to play football?" Kevin asked Katie at recess on Monday.

Katie shook her head. "I already promised Mandy and the Emmas that I would jump rope."

"Maybe they'll want to play football instead?" Kevin asked her.

"I don't think so," Katie said. "Why don't you get Jeremy or Manny?"

"None of the guys from class 4B are here," Kevin said. "They're all in the library."

"The library?" Katie asked. "At recess?" That didn't make any sense at all.

Kevin nodded. "It's the only place they can get away from the pom-pom squad," he explained. "There's no cheering allowed in the library. So Suzanne and the rest of the girls are pestering other kids. Just look."

Kevin was right. The 4B squad was cheering for the third-graders who were playing hopscotch.

"Throw that key. Hop to three. Reach the ten. Come back again!"

They also cheered on the second-graders who were playing tag.

"Run, run, run. Don't get hit. Because if you're tagged, you are it."

Katie sighed. "The 4B pom-pom squad is splitting up our whole grade."

"It's different for high school cheerleaders," Emma W. said. "They're cheering for their whole school, not just one grade or one class, the way the pom-pom squad is . . ."

Suddenly, Katie got one of her great ideas. A huge smile flashed across her face. "Emma W., you're a genius!" she exclaimed.

"Thanks," Emma W. answered happily. Then

she paused. "Why am I a genius?" she asked.

"You'll see," Katie said. "I think I know how to make everyone friends again. I just have to get Mr. G.'s permission. Will you guys come with me to talk to him after recess?"

Mandy and the two Emmas all nodded.

* * *

"Mr. G., we think this school needs some spirit," Katie told her teacher a little while later as the kids in her class came back from recess.

"*School* spirit," Emma W. added. "Not just class spirit."

Mr. G. nodded. "There has been a lot of cheering in class 4B lately."

"And nowhere else," Katie said. "That's the problem. We all go to one school. Shouldn't we be cheering about that?"

"It makes perfect sense to me," Mr. G. said.

"That's why we thought the fourth grade could host a pep rally for the whole school," Katie explained. "Every grade would be there.

We could do it in the gym. That's big enough to hold everyone."

"We could have pom-poms, and maybe write a school cheer," Mandy said.

"One that *everyone* could learn," Katie added.

"I think that sounds like a great idea," Mr. G. said. "I'll talk to Principal Kane about it."

As Katie and her friends took their seats, Emma W. whispered to Katie, "Do you think Principal Kane will say yes to a pep rally?"

Katie held up her right hand and crossed her fingers tight.

Chapter 11

The fourth-graders piled into the auditorium on Tuesday morning. But they did not sit together. Class 4A was on the right side of the room. The class 4B pom-pom squad sat in the front row on the left side of the room. And the boys in class 4B sat as far away from the pom-pom girls as possible.

"What do you think this is about?" Katie heard Suzanne ask Miriam.

"I have no clue," Miriam answered.

"Do you think it's something we can do a cheer for?" Becky asked. "Because I've been writing a new one. It's for Jeremy."

"*All* your cheers are for Jeremy," Suzanne

pointed out.

Just then, Mr. G. and Ms. Sweet stood up in front of the kids.

"I bet you dudes are wondering why we've gathered you all together," Mr. G. said. "Well, it's about all the cheering that's been going on around here lately."

"Yeah!" The pom-pom squad began to cheer. They waved their pom-poms in the air.

"We think spirit is a great thing," Ms. Sweet told the kids. "But only when it's done nicely, and not used to hurt other people's feelings."

"Or make them crazy in the bathroom," Sam shouted from the back of the room.

The kids all started to laugh.

"Exactly," Ms. Sweet said with a smile. "There's a time and a place for cheering."

"And that time and place is next Monday in the school gym," Mr. G. said. "Because that's when we're going to have the first ever Cherrydale Elementary all-school pep rally!"

"Hosted by the whole fourth grade!" Ms. Sweet added.

The fourth grade didn't usually get to be in charge of an event for the whole school. This was a very big deal.

"You dudes are all going to have to work together to pull this off," Mr. G. said. "You're going to have to make enough pom-poms for everyone in the school. And you'll have to write a school cheer which you will teach the whole school."

"And since you'll be working so hard, there won't be any time for cheering in the halls or in the cafeteria or on the playground," Ms. Sweet said. She smiled at Sam. "Or outside the bathrooms."

"From now on, the only cheering coming from the fourth grade will be at next week's pep rally," Mr. G. said. "Got it?"

"Got it," the kids all answered at once.

"And are you ready to show some real school spirit?" Mr. G. asked.

"YEAH!" the fourth-graders shouted.

Katie smiled. That was the first thing the fourth-graders had agreed on in a long time.

★ ★ ★

"I can't believe your sister got the high school to lend us their mascot costume for our pep rally," Katie said as she, Emma W., Suzanne, Jeremy, Becky, Miriam, Kadeem, and Kevin all sat together at a table making pom-poms out of trash bags on Friday afternoon.

"They were so happy you gave them the idea

of turning their pyramid into a *V* for victory that they were glad to help us," Emma W. said. "And it's usually a shorter kid who wears the mascot suit, so one of us should be able to wear it with no problem."

"I think you should wear it," Katie told Emma W. "After all, you're the one with the sister who's a cheerleader."

"No, *you* should wear it," Emma W. told Katie. "You were the one who straightened everything out for Lacey."

"I can settle this," Suzanne told the girls. "*I'll* wear the mascot costume."

"You?" Becky asked. "Why you?"

"Because I started cheerleading at Cherrydale Elementary," she said.

"Actually, I think Emma W. and Katie started it," Miriam said.

"The pom-pom squad was my idea," Suzanne said. "It was such a great idea, now the whole school is having a pep rally. Don't you think I should be rewarded?"

Katie sighed. *Great* wasn't exactly the word she'd use to describe the idea for the 4B pom-pom squad. Annoying, maybe. But not great.

"Suzanne, I don't think you're going to like the costume," Emma W. said slowly.

"Emma W.'s right," Katie added. "It's not really your style."

Suzanne rolled her eyes. "Nice try," she said. "But you two are not going to be able to talk me out of this one. I'm wearing the mascot costume, and that's that."

Chapter 12

"A *squid?*" Suzanne's voice scaled up nervously as she took the costume out of its box. It was Monday morning, right before the pep rally. "They're the Cherrydale High School *Squids?*"

Katie and Emma W. nodded. "Yep." They were all in the girls' bathroom.

Suzanne looked at the costume. She fingered each of the fuzzy tentacles, and stared at the bulging squid eyes.

"That mascot was a big hit at the state competition," Emma W. assured Suzanne. "Everyone thought it was really funny."

Suzanne made a face.

Katie understood why Suzanne didn't seem thrilled. Funny was never the look Suzanne was going for. On the other hand, Katie also knew Suzanne would never give someone else the chance to wear the costume. Not after she'd made such a big fuss about it.

"Well, the tentacles are a nice shade of red, anyway," Suzanne said. "I guess I could wear it."

"How did Lacey's squad do?" Katie asked.

"They came in second," Emma W. told her. "That's the highest they've ever placed. And the pyramid routine was a real hit."

Katie smiled proudly. Now she just hoped that her idea for an all-school pep rally would be a hit, too.

Mandy and Miriam walked into the girls' bathroom.

"We just finished giving out the pom-poms," Mandy told them. "Suzanne, you have to hurry up. We need to get started."

"Why?" Emma W. asked her.

"A few of the second-graders are trying to use their pom-poms as swords," Miriam explained. "Principal Kane is worried someone's going to poke an eye out."

"That would be awful," Katie said.

"You're telling me," Suzanne said. "Those kids need both eyes to really appreciate me in this costume."

Katie sighed. Somehow Suzanne always managed to focus the attention on herself.

Katie hurried and zipped Suzanne into her squid costume. Then the girls helped lead her out into the gym.

As soon as the kids saw Suzanne they all began to laugh. "What is that octopus doing here?" Katie heard some first-grader ask.

Suzanne stopped in her tracks. For a minute, Katie thought she was going to run out of the gym. But Suzanne didn't run. Instead, she turned to the first-grader and said, "I'm not an octopus. Don't you know a squid when you see one?"

Katie gulped. That was kind of harsh. How was a first-grader supposed to know the difference between an octopus and a squid?

The first-grader looked upset. No way was Suzanne going to ruin this pep rally. Quickly, Katie leaped up and raced to Suzanne's side.

"That's right, this is the Cherrydale squid!" Katie cheered. "He's the high school's mascot, and now he's our mascot, too. Let's hear it: Squids rule! Squids rule!"

A moment later, the whole school was shouting along with Katie. "Squids rule! Squids rule!"

Phew. That had been close. And then, suddenly, Katie felt a cool breeze blowing on the back of her neck. Oh no! Had the magic wind returned? Katie didn't want to switcheroo into

anybody else. Not now. Not in front of everyone in the whole school. Not when she was having so much fun.

For a minute, Katie thought she was going to burst into tears. But then she turned around. Whew! So many of the first-graders were waving their pom-poms that they had made a breeze. Emma W.'s hair was blowing a little.

Hooray! Katie was going to stay Katie! At least for now.

She was so happy, she felt like cheering.

And that was just what she did. Katie cheered along with the rest of the fourth grade—because no one in the whole school had more school spirit than Katie Kazoo!

"Who's got spirit? We've got spirit. Stand on up and let us hear it! Go Cherrydale! We are cool and we are great! We're the best, we really rate! Listen up 'cause we're not fools. When it comes to schools, Cherrydale rules! GO CHERRYDALE ELEMENTARY!"

About the Author

Nancy Krulik is the author of more than 150 books for children and young adults, including three *New York Times* best sellers. She lives in New York City with her husband, composer Daniel Burwasser, and their children, Amanda and Ian. When she's not busy writing the Katie Kazoo, Switcheroo series, Nancy loves swimming, reading, and going to the movies.

★ ★ ★

About the Illustrators

John & Wendy have illustrated all of the Katie Kazoo books, but when they're not busy drawing Katie and her friends, they like to paint, take photographs, travel, and play music in their rock 'n' roll band. They live and work in Brooklyn, New York.